First published 1989 by Walker Books Ltd, 87 Vauxhall Walk, London SE11 5HJ

This edition published 2021

2 4 6 8 10 9 7 5 3 1

Text © 1989 John Yeoman
Illustrations © 1989 Quentin Blake

The right of John Yeoman and Quentin Blake to be identified as author and illustrator respectively
of this work has been asserted by them in accordance with the Copyright, Designs and Patents Act 1988

This book has been typeset in Bembo

Printed in China

British Library Cataloguing in Publication Data:
a catalogue record for this book is available from the British Library

ISBN 978-1-4063-9592-1

www.walker.co.uk

X080768

This Walker book belongs to:

_____

_____

Old Mother Hubbard's Dog

Takes Up Sport

John Yeoman
Quentin Blake

WALKER BOOKS
AND SUBSIDIARIES
LONDON · BOSTON · SYDNEY · AUCKLAND

Said Old Mother Hubbard, while combing her hair,
"I don't understand you at all:
You just laze around in a comfortable chair,
While normal dogs play with a ball."

Then, three minutes later
    (it might have been four),
She saw that her troublesome pet
Was playing at tennis against the back door,
With a line of wet clothes for a net.

Said Old Mother Hubbard, "I'm wholly confused!
What is this? It doesn't make sense."
But meanwhile, the dog, looking faintly amused,
Kept pole-vaulting over the fence.

He then got a football, and kicked – with a thud! –
And headed it, higher and higher.
He came in, exhausted, all covered in mud,
And took a hot bath by the fire.

Thought Old Mother Hubbard, while cleaning the bath,
"There's nothing that dog wouldn't dare:
He's speeding on roller-skates right down the path
And doing quick spins in the air."

He went for a jog, and he then had a try
At the long jump, the high jump – the lot.
He picked up the piglets from out of the sty
And practised at putting the shot.

A little while after, the poor woman froze;
She whispered, "What is he at now?"
The dog was improving his javelin throws
And giving a fright to her cow.

She beckoned him in, barely able to speak,
And settled him down in her lap;
She sighed, "All this energy leaves me quite weak.
I'll teach you a quiet game of Snap."

The Adventures of Old Mother Hubbard's Dog

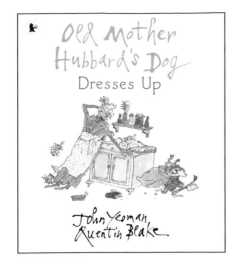

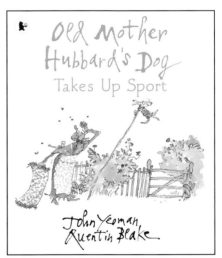

Also illustrated by Quentin Blake

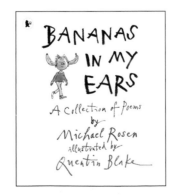

Available from all good booksellers

www.walker.co.uk